WOLF'S MAGNIFICENT MASTER PLAN

Melanie Williamson

Hodder Children's Books

A division of Hachette Children's Books

'Arraghhh!'

Wolf sat at his kitchen table
wincing in terrible pain.

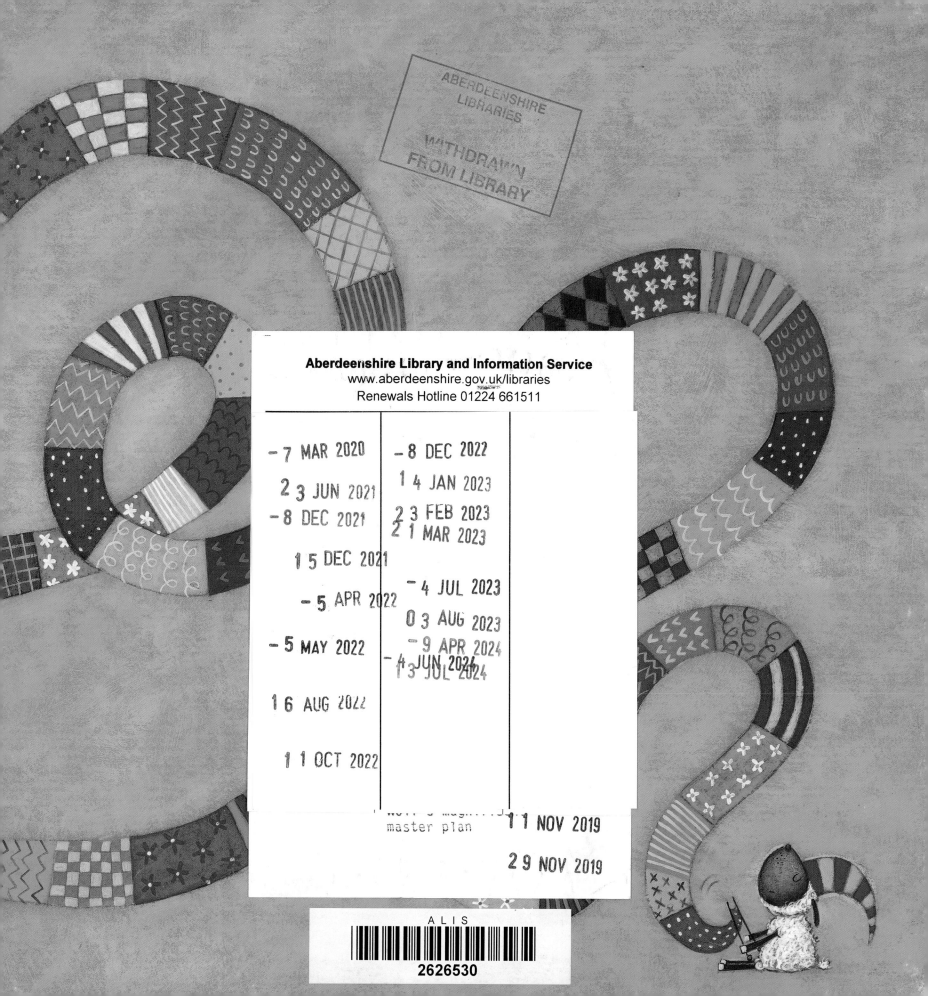

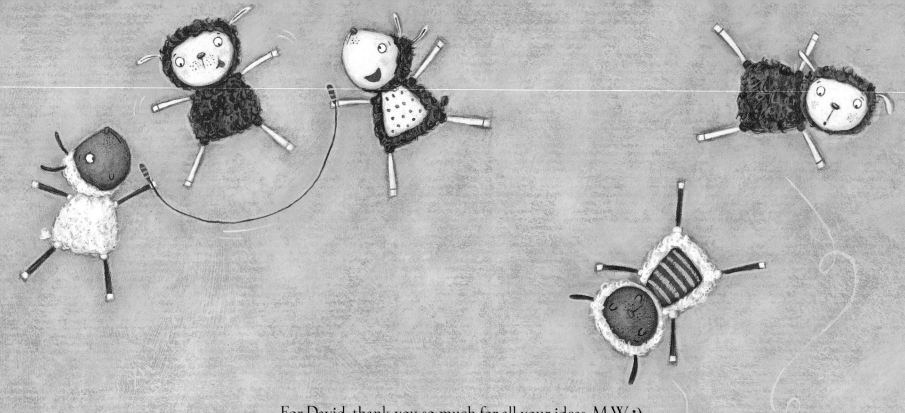

For David, thank you so much for all your ideas. M.W :)

Wolf's Magnificent Master Plan
First published in hardback in 2008
by Hodder Children's Books

Copyright © Melanie Williamson 2008

Hodder Children's Books
338 Euston Road
London, NW1 3BH

Hodder Children's Books Australia
Level 17/207 Kent Street
Sydney, NSW 2000

A catalogue record of this book is available from the British Library.

ISBN: 978 0 340 95059 3

Printed in China

Hodder Children's Books
is a division of Hachette Children's Books.
An Hachette Livre UK Company.

www.hachettelivre.co.uk

His last rotten tooth was
throbbing and he longed
to eat something, anything,
other than soup!

Oh, what he would give
to snack on a juicy, plump
lamb chop!

Now, new teeth don't come cheap so Wolf had to come up
with a marvellous money-making scheme.
He would get the lambs to knit jumpers,
using their own wool, which
he would sell in his shop.
It was a perfect
cunning plan.

'What a clever
Wolf I am!' he
splurted, admiring
his master plan.

Next morning, Wolf set off to the lambs' den to put part-one of his magnificent master plan into action.

'If you knit the jumpers, I will sell them in my shop and soon we will all be rich!' said Wolf slyly.

'But we don't know how to knit,' said the smallest black lamb.

'And, even if we did, we wouldn't work for *you*,' said the brave little spotty one.

Wolf trudged home, his tail between his legs. There must be a way of persuading the lambs to work for him...

Wolf's house

TICK-TOCK! TICK-TOCK! TICK-TOCK! TICK-TOCK! TICK-TOCK! TICK-TOCK! TICK-TOCK! TICK-TOCK! TICK-TOCK! TICK-TOCK!

As he sat waiting for another tin of soup to simmer, Wolf suddenly had an idea! 'If the lambs won't work for me, then I will hypnotise them in to it!' he sniggered.

That night, as the lambs softly snoozed, Wolf sneaked into their den and hid a tape in the clock on the wall.

'Wolf is your friend.

You really like Wolf. You would love to work for Wolf...

On and on the tape played,
until the sun rose and the lambs
stumbled in a trance out of bed.

Within a few days, Wolf had his very own production factory, making woolly jumpers of every shape, size and pattern imaginable!

Shear

Spin

There were lambs furiously shearing,
spinning and knitting wool
all over the place!

Bertie Badger's Bakery

It wasn't long before Wolf had sold enough jumpers to put part-two of his master plan into action and buy a brand-new set of razor-sharp teeth!

'Oh, I am the most handsome, cleverest Wolf I ever met,' he said, admiring his new look.

+FLOSSY FOX'S PHARMACY+

OPEN

Wolf was so busy showing-off his shiny new teeth that he forgot all about the lambs back at the factory...

At the end of the working day, the little stripy lamb took a huge pile of knitting to Wolf's shop.

But the little lamb couldn't see where he was going and tripped straight over the empty money jar on the floor!

CRASH!

WOLF'S MAGNIFICENT MASTER PLAN

friends

wool

SHOP

£

teeth

yum yum!

As the little lamb came out of his trance he stared straight up at Wolf's master plan!

The little stripy lamb ran out of the door and all the way back to the factory. His loud screams woke the other lambs from their hypnotic spell.

'Wolf has gone out to buy s-some, n-new t-teeth, to eat us!' stuttered the little lamb.

Shocked faces filled the fields.

'Wolf is not the only
one who can be
conniving,' said
the little brown lamb
with a smile.

As the night stars twinkled, Wolf
finally skipped back home. His new
teeth gleamed in the moonlight.

'Lamp chops or lamb burgers?'
he salivated, thinking of his tasty supper.
'Rare, medium or well-done?
With mint or ketchup?'

Meanwhile, on the other side of the hill, the lambs had been knitting furiously all afternoon.

Wolf slyly scampered into
the lambs' den and crept up
to the first bunk.

His tummy rumbled
and his mouth watered
as he dived in teeth first!

CRACK!

SPLIT!

'Arragghh!'

Wolf's teeth shattered
and crumbled to the floor.

'We fooled you! We fooled you!'
cried the lambs, jumping out from
under the bunks.

They had knitted
a fake lamb and
stuffed it with bricks!

Wolf was so embarrassed that the little lambs had outwitted him that he ran away as fast as his hairy legs would carry him.

1.
To never
trust
a wolf.

The lambs never saw Wolf again and from that day on they always remembered three very important things: